Titles in this series

Railway Series, No. 15

THE TWIN ENGINES

by
THE REV. W. AWDRY

with illustrations by
JOHN T. KENNEY

EGMONT

EGMONT

We bring stories to life

First published in Great Britain in 1960
This edition published 2011
by Egmont UK Limited
239 Kensington High Street, London W8 6SA

HiT entertainment

ISBN 978 1 4052 0345 6

1 3 5 7 9 10 8 6 4 2

Printed and bound in China

DEAR FRIENDS,

The Fat Controller has just been having a Disturbing Time! He ordered one goods engine from Scotland, and was surprised to receive two!

They had both lost their numbers, and no one knew which was which. So he didn't know which engine to keep.

THE AUTHOR

'Hullo Twins!'

MORE and more people travelled on the Fat Controller's Railway. More and more ships came to the harbours. Everyone had to work very hard indeed.

The trucks complained bitterly; but then, trucks always do, and no one takes much notice.

The coaches complained too. No sooner had they arrived with one train, than they had to go out again with fresh passengers as another.

"We don't know whether we're coming or going," they protested. "We feel *quite* distracted."

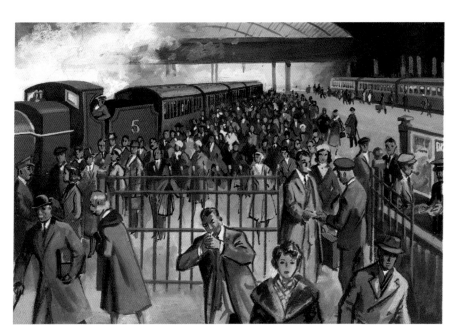

"No one can say," grumbled Henry, "that we're afraid of hard work, but . . ."

". . . we draw the line at goods trains," finished Gordon.

"Dirty trucks, dirty sidings. Ugh!" put in James.

"What are you boiler-aching about?" asked Duck. "I remember on the Great Western . . ."

"That tin-pot railway . . ."

"Tin-pot indeed! Let me tell you . . ."

"Silence!" ordered a well-known voice. "Let me tell you that an engine for goods work will arrive from Scotland tomorrow."

The news was received with acclamation.

The Fat Controller stared. "Did you say *two* engines, Inspector?"

"Yes, Sir."

"Then send the other back at once."

"Certainly Sir, but which?"

The Fat Controller stared again. "Engines have numbers, Inspector," he explained patiently. "We bought No. 57646. Send the other one back."

"Quite so Sir, but there is a difficulty."

"What *do* you mean?"

"The two engines are exactly alike Sir, and have no numbers. They say they lost them on the way."

The Fat Controller seized his hat. "We'll soon settle that nonsense," he said grimly.

The two engines greeted him cheerfully.

"I hear you've lost your numbers," he said. "How did that happen?"

"They maun hae slyly slippit aff Sirr. Ye ken hoo it is." The engines spoke in chorus.

"I know. Accidentally on purpose."

The twins looked pained. "Sirr! Ye wadnae be thinkin' we lost them on purrpose?"

"I'm not so sure," said the Fat Controller. "Now then, which of you is 57646?"

"That, Sirr, is juist what we canna mind."

The Fat Controller looked at their solemn faces. He turned away. He seemed to have difficulty with his own.

He swung round again. "What are your names?"

"Donal an' Douggie, Sirr."

"Good!" he said. "Then your Controller can tell me which of you is which."

"Och! Ye'll no get muckle help fae him, Sirr."

"Why?"

"He disna ken oor names Sirr. Hoo cud he? We only gien oorsels names when we lost oor nummers."

"One of you," said the Fat Controller, "is playing truant. I shall find him out and send him home. Inspector," he ordered, "give these engines numbers, and set them to work."

He walked sternly away.

The Missing Coach

SOON workmen came to give the twins their numbers. Donald was 9 and Douglas 10. When the men went away, they were left alone in the Shed.

"Ye may hae noticed, Douggie, that yon penters forgot somethin'."

"What did they forget?"

"They pented braw new nummers on oor tenders, but they put nane on uz." Donald winked broadly at his twin.

"Ye mean," grinned Douglas, "that we can . . ."

"Juist that," chuckled Donald. "Haud yer wheesht. Here's the Inspector."

"Now 9 and 10," smiled the Inspector, "here's Duck. He'll show you round before you start work."

The twins enjoyed themselves, and were soon friends with Duck. They didn't mind what they did. They tackled goods trains and coaches easily; for, once the twins had shunted them, trucks knew better than to try any tricks.

"We like it fine here," said Donald.

"That's good," smiled Duck, "but take my tip, watch out for Gordon, Henry and James. They're sure to try some nonsense."

"Dinna fash yersel," chuckled Douglas. "We'll suin settle them."

Donald and Douglas had deep-toned whistles.

"They sound like buses," said Gordon.

"Or ships," sniggered Henry.

"Tug-boat Annie!" laughed Gordon. "Ha! Ha!"

Donald and Douglas cruised quietly up, one on each side. "Ye wadnae be makkin' fun o' uz wad ye noo?" asked Donald.

Gordon and Henry jumped. They glanced nervously from side to side.

"Er, no," said Gordon.

"No, no, certainly not," said Henry.

"That's fine," said Douglas. "Noo juist mind the baith o' ye, and keep it that wey."

That was the way Gordon and Henry kept it!

Every day, punctually at 3.30, Gordon steams in with the Express. It is called "The Wild Nor' Wester", and is full of people from England, Wales, and Scotland. There is also a special coach for passengers travelling to places on Thomas' Branch Line.

When the other coaches are taken away empty, engines have to remember to shunt the special coach to the bay platform. It does not wait there long. Thomas, with Annie and Clarabel, comes hurrying from the junction to fetch it. Thomas is very proud of his Special Coach.

One afternoon Douglas helped Duck in the Yard while Donald waited to take a goods train to the other end of the line. As Duck was busy arranging Donald's trucks, Douglas offered to take away Gordon's coaches.

Douglas was enjoying himself, when an awful thought struck him. "I hope the Fat Controller disna find oot I shudna be here. I cudna abide gooin' back." He worried so much over this that he forgot about Thomas' special coach.

He pushed it with the others into the carriage siding, then ambled along to join Donald at the water column. As he went, Thomas scampered by whistling cheerfully.

Soon Thomas came fussing. "Where's my coach?"

"Cooch?" asked Donald. "What cooch?"

"My special coach, that Gordon brings for me. It's gone. I must find it." He bustled away.

"Losh sakes!" said Douglas. "I maun hae stowed the special cooch wi the ithers."

"D'ye see that?" exclaimed Donald's Driver. A mob of angry passengers erupted from the siding. "They're complainin' tae the Fat Controller. He'll be comin' here next."

"Noo listen," said Douglas' Driver. We'll chainge tenders. Then awa' wi ye, Donal, an' tak yon Guids. Dinna fash aboot uz. Quick noo! Dae as I say."

24

The Fat Controller and three passengers walked towards them; but Donald, with Douglas' tender (10), was out and away with the Goods before they came near. Douglas and his Driver waited with innocent expressions.

"Ah!" said the Fat Controller, "No. 9, and why have you not taken the Goods?"

"My tender is awa' Sirr." The Driver showed him the tender, still uncoupled.

"I see, some defect no doubt. Tell me, why did No. 10 leave so quickly?"

"Mebbe Sirr," put in Douglas, "he saw ye comin' an' thocht he was late."

"Hm," said the Fat Controller.

He turned to the passengers. "Here, Gentlemen, are the facts. No. 10 has been shunting the Yard. Your coach disappeared. We investigate. No. 10 – er – disappears too. You can draw your conclusions. Please accept my apologies. The matter will be investigated. Good afternoon, Gentlemen."

The Fat Controller watched them till they climbed the station ramp. His shoulders twitched; he wiped his eyes. Douglas wondered if he was crying. He was not.

He swung round suddenly. "Douglas", he rapped, "why are you masquerading with Donald's tender?"

Break Van

THE FAT CONTROLLER scolded both engines severely.

"There must be no more tricks," he said. "I shall be watching you both. I have to decide which of you is to stay." He strode away.

The twins looked glum. Neither wanted to stay without the other. They said so.

"Then what is tae dae?" wondered Douglas.

"Och!" said Donald. "Each maun be aye guid as ither. Syne he'll hae tae keep uz baith."

Their plan was good; but they had reckoned without a spiteful Brake van.

The van had taken a dislike to Douglas. Things always went wrong when he had to take it out. Then his trains were late, and he was blamed. Douglas began to worry.

"Ye're a muckle nuisance," said Donald one day. "It's tae leave ye behind I'd be wantin'."

"You can't," said the van, "I'm essential."

"Och are ye?" Donald burst out. "Ye're naethin' but a screechin' an' a noise when a's said an' done. Spite Douggie wad ye? Tak that."

"Oh! Oh! Oh!" cried the van.

"Haud yer wheesht," said Donald severely. "There's mair comin' syne ye misbehave."

The van behaved better after that. Douglas' trains were punctual, and the twins felt happier.

Then Donald had an accident. He backed into a siding. The rails were slippery. He couldn't stop in time, and crashed through the buffers into a signal box.

One moment the Signalman was standing on the stairs; the next, he was sitting on the coal in Donald's tender. He was most annoyed.

"You clumsy great engine," he stormed, "now you must stay there. You've jammed my points. It serves you right for spoiling my nice new signal box."

The Fat Controller was cross too. "I am disappointed, Donald," he said. "I did not expect such – er – such clumsiness from you. I had decided to send Douglas back and keep you."

"I'm sorry, Sirr," but Donald didn't say what he was sorry for. We know, don't we?

"I should think so too," went on the Fat Controller indignantly. "You have upset my Arrangements. It is Most Inconvenient. Now James will have to help with the goods work, while you have your tender mended. James won't like that."

The Fat Controller was right. James grumbled dreadfully.

"Ony wan wad think," said Douglas, "that Donal had his accident on purrpose. I heard tell," he went on, "aboot an engine an' some tar wagons."

Gordon and Henry chuckled.

"Shut up!" said James. "It's not funny."

"Weel, weel, weel!" said Douglas innocently. "Shairly Jeames it wasna you? Ye dinna say!"

James didn't say. He was sulky next morning, and wouldn't steam properly. When at last he did start, he bumped the trucks hard.

"He's cross," sniggered the spiteful Brake van. "We'll try to make him crosser still!"

"Hold back!" whispered the van to the trucks.

"Hold back!" giggled the trucks to each other.

James did his best, but he was exhausted when they reached Edward's station. Luckily Douglas was there.

"Help me up the hill please," panted James. "These trucks are playing tricks."

"We'll show them," said Douglas grimly.

"ComeonComeonCOMEON," puffed James crossly.

"Get MOV-in' you! Get MOV-in' you!" puffed Douglas from behind.

Slowly but surely the snorting engines forced the unwilling trucks up the hill.

But James was losing steam. "I can't do it. I can't do it," he panted.

"LAE IT TAE ME! LAE IT TAE ME!" shouted Douglas. He pushed and he puffed so furiously that sparks leapt from his funnel.

"Ooer!" groaned the van. "I wish I'd never thought of this." It was squeezed between Douglas and the trucks. "Go on! Go on!" it screamed; but they took no notice.

The Guard was anxious. "Go steady!" he yelled to Douglas. "The van's breaking."

It was too late. The Guard jumped as the van collapsed. He landed safely on the side of the line.

"I might have known it would be Douglas!"

"I'm sorry Sirr. Mebbe I was clumsy, but I *wadna* be beaten by yon tricksie van."

"I see," said the Fat Controller.

Edward brought workmen to clear the mess.

"Douglas was grand Sir," he said. "James had no steam left, but Douglas worked hard enough for three. I heard him from my yard."

"Two would have been enough," said the Fat Controller drily. "I want to be fair, Douglas," he went on. "I admire your determination, but . . . I don't know, I really don't know."

He turned and walked thoughtfully away.

The Deputation

"HE'LL send uz awa' for shair, Donal."

"I'm thinkin' ye're richt there, Douggie. The luck's aye been agin uz. An engine disna ken what tae dae for the best."

Snow came early that year. It was heavier than usual. It stayed too, and choked the lines. Most engines hate snow. Donald and Douglas were used to it. They knew what to do. Their Drivers spoke to the Inspector, and they were soon coupled back to back, with a van between their tenders. Then, each with a snow plough on their fronts, they set to work.

They puffed busily backwards and forwards patrolling the line. Generally the snow slipped away easily, but sometimes they found deeper drifts.

Then they would charge them again and again, snorting, slipping, puffing, panting, till they had forced their way through.

Presently they came to a drift which was larger than most. They charged it, and were backing for another try. There was a feeble whistle, people waved and shouted.

"Losh sakes, Donal, it's Henry! Dinna fash yersel, Henry. Bide a wee. We'll hae ye oot!"

* * * * * *

The Fat Controller was returning soon. The twins were glum. "He'll send uz back for shair," they said.

"It's a shame!" sympathised Percy.

"A lot of nonsense about a signal box," grumbled Gordon. "Too many of those, if you ask me."

"That Brake van too," put in James. "Good riddance. That's what I say."

"They were splendid in the snow," added Henry. "It isn't fair." They all agreed that Something Must Be Done, but none knew what.

One day Percy talked to Edward about it.

"What you need," said Edward, "is a Deputation." He explained what that was.

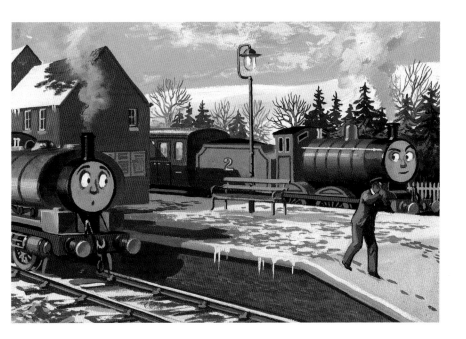

Percy ran back quickly. "Edward says we need a Depotstation," he told the others.

"Of course," said Gordon, "the question is . . ."

" . . . what is a desperation?" asked Henry.

"It's when engines tell the Fat Controller something's wrong, and ask him to put it right."

"Did you say *tell* the Fat Controller?" asked Duck thoughtfully. There was a long silence.

"I propose," said Gordon at last, "that Percy be our – er – hum – disputation."

"HI!" squeaked Percy. "I can't."

"Rubbish Percy," said Henry. "It's easy."

"That's settled then," said Gordon.

Poor Percy wished it wasn't!

"Hullo, Percy! It's nice to be back."

Percy jumped. Some trucks went flying.

"Er y-y-yes Sir, please Sir."

"You look nervous, Percy. What's the matter?"

"Please Sir, they've made me a Desperation Sir. To Speak to You Sir. I don't like it Sir."

The Fat Controller pondered. "Do you mean a Deputation, Percy?" he asked.

"Yes Sir, please Sir. It's Donald and Douglas Sir. They say, Sir, that if you send them away, Sir, they'll be turned into Scrap, Sir. That'd be dreadful, Sir. Please Sir, don't send them away, Sir. They're nice engines, Sir."

"Thank you, Percy. That will do." He walked away.

"I had a – er – deputation yesterday," said the Fat Controller. "I understand your feelings but I do *not* approve of interference." He paused impressively. "Donald and Douglas, I hear that your work in the snow was good. What colour paint would you like?"

The twins were surprised. "Blue, Sirr, please."

"Very well. But your names will be painted on you. We'll have no more 'mistakes'."

"Thankye Sirr. Dis this mean that the baith o' uz . . . ?"

The Fat Controller smiled. "It means . . ."

But the rest of his speech was drowned in a delighted chorus of cheers and whistles.